Robert C. Waterston

Address on the Life and Character of Thomas Sherwin

Robert C. Waterston

Address on the Life and Character of Thomas Sherwin

ISBN/EAN: 9783337396695

Printed in Europe, USA, Canada, Australia, Japan

Cover: Foto ©Andreas Hilbeck / pixelio.de

More available books at **www.hansebooks.com**

ADDRESS

ON THE LIFE AND CHARACTER OF

THOMAS SHERWIN,

BY R. C. WATERSTON,

DELIVERED FEBRUARY 16, 1870,

BEFORE THE

ENGLISH HIGH SCHOOL ASSOCIATION,

THE

Members of the School Board,

AND TEACHERS OF THE PUBLIC SCHOOLS OF BOSTON.

BOSTON:

ALFRED MUDGE & SON, PRINTERS, 34 SCHOOL STREET.

1870.

CITY OF BOSTON.

In School Committee, March 8, 1870.

Ordered, That twelve hundred copies of Mr. Waterston's Eulogy on Thomas Sherwin, late head-master of the English High School, delivered before the English High School Association, be printed for the use of this Board, and for distribution among the teachers of the High and Grammar Schools.

Attest:

BARNARD CAPEN,
Secretary.

ENGLISH HIGH SCHOOL ASSOCIATION.

, *Resolved*, That the thanks of the English High School Association be hereby tendered by the government to the Rev. R. C. Waterston for his able and eloquent address on the life and character of Thomas Sherwin, in the beauty and truth of which we shall always recognize the most valued memorial of our departed teacher.

Resolved, That a copy of the address be requested for publication.

WM. H. MORIARTY,
Secretary.

March 9, 1870.

⁎ A paper was also received requesting that the Address should be printed, signed by the Masters of the High and Grammar Schools of the city, dated March 7 1870.

TO

The Members of the School Board;

THE GRADUATES

OF THE HIGH SCHOOL;

AND

INSTRUCTORS IN THE PUBLIC SCHOOLS OF BOSTON

THIS RECORD

OF

A BELOVED AND FAITHFUL TEACHER

IS

RESPECTFULLY

DEDICATED.

THE following address, prepared at the request of the English High School Association, was delivered in the Horticultural Hall, on the evening of the 16th of February, 1870, before a large audience, among whom were the members of the School Committee and both branches of the City Government, the teachers of the public schools of Boston, and a large number of the past graduates of the English High School. The platform was adorned with azaleas and other plants, generously contributed by Mr. Sherwin's early friend, Marshall P. Wilder. A fine portrait of Mr. Sherwin was also beautifully decorated with flowers. On the platform around the speaker were his Excellency Governor Claflin, his Honor Mayor Shurtleff, the Hon. Charles Francis Adams, the Hon. Marshall P. Wilder, George B. Emerson, John D. Philbrick, a number of the college classmates of Mr. Sherwin, and other distinguished men. Mr. Gaffield, the President of the English High School Association, presided, and opened the meeting with appropriate remarks. Prayer was offered by the Rev. S. K. Lothrop, D. D.

A quartette and chorus from Mendelssohn — "Ye Sons of Israel," and the " Chorus of Angels," from Costa's oratorio of " Eli " — were sung during the services by a number of the young ladies from the Girls' High and Normal School, under the direction of Julius Eichberg. Both of the selections were peculiarly appropriate to the occasion, and were rendered with great taste and accuracy. The services were closed by a Benediction.

A portion of the address, as now printed, was necessarily omitted in the delivery.

INTRODUCTORY REMARKS

BY

THOMAS GAFFIELD,

President of the English High School Association.

Ladies and Gentlemen, and Fellow-members of the
English High School Association:

We have assembled on no ordinary occasion. For the
first time in the history of our city, do we behold His Excellency the Governor, His Honor the Mayor, the members of
the government, and the school committee, the able teachers
of our public schools, and many of our most distinguished citizens, uniting with aged classmates and early and later pupils
in a tribute of respect to the memory of a beloved and honored schoolmaster. As one of those pupils of thirty years
ago, may I be permitted in a word to say, that, modest and
unassuming as he was, he yet realized the dignity and honor
of his profession, and forty years and more of faithful and
devoted service in educating the youth of Boston at the English High School, and in moulding the characters of men,
who, in almost every land on earth, have become distinguished in mercantile, professional or political life, entitle

him to the gratitude of all our fellow-citizens. His was that rare combination of the Christian gentleman and teacher, which not only educated the minds of his pupils, and made them scholars, but warmed their hearts and made them men.

It was this, my fellow-schoolmates, which made the fondness of school-boy days ripen into the friendship and love of manhood, and gave us such delight whenever we took his hand, or heard his words, or beheld his beautiful face, which grew more and more into a benediction, as he advanced in wisdom and goodness and years.

Shall we not appropriately honor his blessed memory, as the memorial committee have decided to do, by embodying in marble those strong, yet loving features, and placing them within the walls of the old school-house, or the new one, which ought soon to be built, with a tablet inscribed with some simple story of his virtues, to be an inspiration to duty and fidelity to teachers and pupils in all coming time. Shall we not equally honor him, as we intend to do, by raising a fund to establish a Sherwin scholarship in the Institute of Technology, in whose foundation he took the warmest interest, and for whose subsequent and remarkably successful growth he labored to the end of his days.

It is most fitting that the young ladies of the Girls' High and Normal School, who themselves have mourned the departure of an honored teacher, should come this evening, as it were, to shed a tear and chant a requiem over the fresher grave of our sainted friend.

And it is well that we should all, honored rulers and merchants, teachers and pupils, fellow-townsmen and friends, spend together a quiet evening hour in listening to the story of an earthly life, which began in cheerful industry, continued for threescore years and ten in active Christian usefulness, and then — as we all remember, at the close of a lovely summer day, when the sun was sinking beneath the horizon, and casting its glorious light behind — passed on, gently and peacefully blending with the life of the angels above, to send back to the eye of spiritual vision, from day to day, its radiance of heavenly beauty for countless years to come. That we may have a fitting memorial of such a life, your committee have invited to address us this evening one of the most accomplished graduates of our school, one who truly loved Mr. Sherwin, as we all loved him, and who has poured his whole soul into his tribute of reverence and affection. How well he knew him, how much he loved him, and how much his love and reverence were deepened by the study of the early and later life of our honored teacher, we shall all realize when we listen to his words, from which I will no longer detain you. I have the pleasure of introducing to you the Rev. R. C. Waterston, a member of the graduating class of 1828.

2

ADDRESS.

AMONG the teachers of New England, probably no one was more truly beloved and honored than Thomas Sherwin. This was not owing to any effort on his part to attract observation, for, in the most unobtrusive manner, he devoted himself to his special duties; neither was it the result of any one quality, developed in an inordinate degree; rather did it proceed from that remarkable completeness of character, and that well-adjusted balance of all his powers, which gave symmetry and beauty to his whole moral and intellectual nature; combined with which, he united widely gathered knowledge, a thorough mastery of whatever subject he had investigated, and the conscientious use of all he was, and all he knew, for the advantage of others. These traits, with his unselfish disposition and genial spirit, won for him universal regard, and made him, as competent judges on every side agreed, one of the leading educators of his time,— a worthy model for the encouragement and emulation of all progressive minds.

Natural it is that every teacher should feel an honest pride in the thought of him. Such a man ennobles and elevates the profession to which he belongs. The whole community of which he is a part is a sharer in his acquirements. Justice demands that we should give expression to the respect we cherish. The places which once knew him, know him no more; yet will his memory give new sanctity to those duties to which he consecrated his life. Not to eulogize with exaggerated praise, but to consider the simple truth, have we come together. A life like his needs only to be seen as it really was. A career so identified with quiet duty, cannot, in the nature of things, present startling facts; yet events, however unpretending, and though in some degree familiar, will not be wholly devoid of interest, associated as they are with the history and development of such a character.

Thomas Sherwin was born on the 26th of March, 1799, at Westmoreland, a lovely region on the banks of the Connecticut, where the hills of New Hampshire recognize, over the placid river, the distant mountains of Vermont. He was the only son of David and Hannah Sherwin; (his mother's maiden name was Pritchard), they were both natives of Boxford, Massachusetts. His father was originally a farmer; later in life he commenced business, but through the dishonesty of his partner he was soon left with but slight means for the support of his family.

Before Thomas was four years of age, his parents removed to New Ipswich, and soon after to the adjoining town of Temple. At the age of seven and a half, he had the misfortune to lose his mother, who died of consumption. In March, 1807, he went to reside with his relative, Dr. James Crombie, a man of professional skill, and highly respected.

At that time, boys were required to make themselves useful. Thomas did this by working in the garden, taking care of the farm stock, sometimes going in search of cattle who had strayed far into the woods, where, in that part of the country, it was then not unfrequent to encounter bears and other wild beasts, whose acquaintance boys generally would not be over-pleased to make under such circumstances. He frequently accompanied the doctor on his round of professional visits, and must have gathered some knowledge of medicine and surgery. Dr. Crombie was a practitioner of more than ordinary ability. Mention is made of his success in the difficult ligature of an artery, considered at that time remarkable. On one occasion, a man was brought to the house with a dislocated arm; the doctor being

absent, Thomas, then quite a youth, put the arm in
its place. Through after life, Mr. Sherwin, in a play-
ful way, would smilingly recall this fact as an evi-
dence of early professional skill! He remained with
Dr. Crombie six years, — from the age of eight to
fourteen, — generally going to the district school
through several weeks of the winter, attending, one
season, a school taught by his sister. For a short
period, he also received instruction at the house of
the Rev. Noah Miles, minister of Temple, from the
clergyman's son, Solomon P. Miles, then a student
at Dartmouth, absent from college on account of ill
health. It is interesting to recall the youthful instructor and his young pupil, and to remember that
both were to be identified, through after years, with
the best days in the history of the English High
School. What a gratification it would have been
to that student from Dartmouth,* could he have anticipated the events of the future, and have known
how widely useful the lad before him was destined
to become. But, though he could not foresee what
we now know, it is a pleasant glimpse which is given
to us of the young teacher during that college vaca-
tion, and the lad coming from the village physician,

---

* Mr. Miles, though at that time connected with Dartmouth, afterwards
entered Harvard College, from which he graduated with honor, in 1819.

to pick up what little instruction he might find. Seeds were then scattered from which would eventually spring a prolific harvest.

My mind goes back forty years, to the time when I was a pupil in the English High School, under Mr. Miles. The thought of his attractive aspect, refined and gentlemanly manners, and thorough scholarship, — all of which won the honor and love of those who enjoyed the privilege of his instructions, — awaken the conviction that even the brief period that Thomas Sherwin was under his influence, in the town of Temple, probably produced a lasting impression upon his whole after career.

But it was not chiefly what was learned at school that constituted the proper education of this part of Thomas Sherwin's experience.

Practical life, with all its activities, was to him education. Working in the garden, upon the farm, taking care of the cattle, carrying messages, attending to matters of business in the workshop and market, compounding medicines, and dealing them out from the doctor's office; at other times in the saddle, riding over the circuit of towns, collecting debts, all this, in a thousand ways, expanded the youthful powers, enlarged his stock of knowledge, and gave an ability to use, to the best advantage, whatever information was acquired. Actual life was a school for him. The characters of the young and the old were to him a study. Work had a meaning. Sprightly and vigorous, he was ready for any duty.

Added to this, he was in the midst of Nature, — open fields, meadows, and hills; the brook and the river; the forest, and the over-arching heavens; with all the phenomena of day and night, and changing seasons, — these were a perpetual resource, demanding of him observation and study. The brown thrush, the blue jay, the red-breasted robin, each had some story for him. The scarlet tanager he would watch, in the month of May, glancing like a flash of light through the forest. For his eye, the oriole hung her nest, and the gossiping bobolink filled the summer air with its merry warblings. All their habits and customs became familiar, while they were dear to his heart as cherished friends. So, also, for him, through the whole vegetable world, every leaf and plant won his notice, from the blue gentian and delicate anemone of spring, to the cardinal flower, like a floating flame, and the aster, and the golden rod of autumn. The thin-leafed willow, the twisted oak, and the towering pine, with their varied characteristics, appealed not in vain to his observant eye. Natural science, not in books, but as God made it, he saw and studied.

Follow him in thought through the lonely pasture and over the open hill. See him threading the banks of the stream, or standing under the shadow of o'er-spreading trees. All these objects, with their marvellous revelations and hidden mysteries, their developments and laws, offered unnumbered suggestions to his thoughtful mind.

So, also, with this rural life was connected simplicity of living, hardy habits, self-reliance, and frugality. Can we say how much of that sturdy vigor and manly perseverance which distinguished his after life had here their origin? How much that love for every created thing — from the smallest atom to the rolling spheres — here dawned into being? How many of those beautiful tastes, pure affections, and heavenly aspirations of his soul were here kindled? Certain it is that, to his latest moment, he was partial to a country life; and natural science, which to him presented always the most powerful attractions, was identified, to a great degree, with the actual objects he had loved to observe and study from his youth.

Doubtless the larger culture which he observed in Dr. Crombie, compared with the average information possessed by the people around, impressed the idea of that mental superiority which comes with knowledge. The very fact that he was in the presence of

3

a more commanding intellect, caused him to be dissatisfied with whatever was narrow and superficial. He, also, must acquire. What barrier should be strong enough inexorably to prevent his progress? And yet there were impediments. How could the requisite opportunities come to him? Alas, impossible! so it naturally appeared.

After he left Dr. Crombie's, the father, to satisfy this strong desire for knowledge on the part of his son, sent him to the Ipswich Academy, — the same institution which has since been endowed by the Appleton family, and which now bears their name. As might be expected, he went to his studies with a hearty will; but, while the formal routine of those days did not answer the demands of his nature, yet even that he could not long continue to enjoy. Pressing need called for practical labor. Gladly would the father have offered his son every possible advantage; but his little property had been swept away, there were five daughters to be cared for, and the son must work. Feeling that this was right, with a cheerful heart he entered upon his task.

At Groton, in September, 1813, he was apprenticed to the clothier's trade. The country was at war with Great Britain, and hence the usual supply of foreign cloths was cut off. Woollen mills, as they now exist, were unknown on this side of the Atlantic, fabrics were made at the domestic loom; after which they were sent elsewhere for fulling, dyeing, and dressing. Thomas was expected to prepare the dyestuffs, keep up the fires, watch the machinery, a constant and laborious work. He speaks of it as "cloth-dressing, wool-carding, etc., with Messrs. Samuel & Sewell Rockwood." I quote from a manuscript in his own handwriting: "Working intensely in the autumn and winter, moderately in summer, and attending school for about two months annually in spring."

Unwillingness to toil was no part of his nature. Manual labor, pursued with a right spirit, was to him no degradation. That was honorable which subserved high ends. Usefulness to others and self-independence were to him worthy objects. Whatever tended to develop the great industrial resources of a country was always, to his mind, a matter of real interest, and the part which any individual took in it was to that degree praiseworthy. These feelings never forsook him. Laboring men, in proportion to their integrity, were always sure of his regard. Labor to him was never drudgery, for he united with it intellect. He was all observation; means and methods, cause and effect, materials, tissues, fabrics, growth and development,—all these, with quick intelligence, became subjects of thought. This, also, was education, direct and practical; and, beyond doubt, not time wasted, but through life to be of the greatest advantage.

Is it not possible that many may undervalue the uses of practical labor in connection with the process of education? It was the custom among the ancient Hebrews to teach all boys a trade; each one who received Rabbinical culture, in conjunction with his other studies, was obliged to learn some handicraft. Thus bodily exercise was combined with mental effort, and the means of an honorable independence secured. The Jews habitually trained their sons to some useful employment as an indispensable part of their education. In the Talmud it is written, "The wise practice some of the arts, lest they should become dependent upon the charities of others." Rabbi Judah saith: "He that teacheth not his son a trade, doth the same as if he taught him to be a thief." Thus Paul himself was taught; and at Corinth, the most luxurious city of Greece, the Apostle, as we well know, continued for a year and a half laboring at his trade. So far from being ashamed of such toil, he gloried in it. He felt that this work was in him as honorable as preaching upon Mars Hill, or writing epistles to the churches.

It may be questioned whether great advantage might not result if some participation in useful labor were combined with intellectual studies; if, in our schools and colleges, there were opportunities for industrial employments which would develop the physical powers, call forth inventive genius, and give a healthy discipline to both body and mind. It was a wise Spartan precept that "the child should be instructed in the arts which will be useful to the man." And Milton said, "I call that a complete and generous education which fits a man to perform justly, skilfully, and magnanimously all the offices, private and public, of peace and war."

Such was the education, not in the school, but out of it, that Providence provided for Thomas Sherwin. By it he gained an experience he could never have extracted from books. Nothing effeminate, but a strong, courageous manliness was to come from such discipline.

I have made inquiries of those who knew him at this period, and will offer extracts from one or two communications.

The first is a letter from Groton, by Mrs. Eliza Green, the honored mother of our respected townsman, Dr. Samuel A. Green. She says: "He was refined in all his tastes, and never spent an idle moment.

He often worked at the mill until after ten o'clock at night, and would then read and study for an hour or two. He was always at church, to which he walked three miles."

The following extract is from a letter addressed to me by Capt. Rockwood, a brother of the Rockwoods with whom he served his time. He says: "After the lapse of over half a century, and at my advanced age, many things respecting Thomas Sherwin may have escaped my recollection, but some things I remember perfectly well. His father came with him to have him apprenticed until he should arrive at the age of twenty-one years. He desired to get an education; but his father told him all he could do for him was to give him a trade, and he submitted without a murmur. An apprentice at that time was to be taught all parts belonging to the trade; in this case, to take a piece of raw cloth from the loom, color and dress it ready for the market. His work was quite varied, as there were many parts belonging to the trade. He was to have a certain amount of schooling, and be taught in arithmetic as far as the rule of three, if he should be capable of learning so far! He was to have his board and clothing, which, with his trade, would be all he would receive. With a judgment far superior to those of his years, he soon gained the esteem of his employers, and was looked upon with perfect confidence, which he never betrayed.

"There was no boy about him, — he was a MAN. He was of a contemplative mind, exercising his own judgment, and was never indolent. His idol, if he had one, was his Book. He always had some volume in his pocket, or where he could lay his hand upon it. But, though interested in books, he never neglected his work. While engaged with the machinery, he would sometimes have a few moments to himself, which he always improved in study. In this way he mastered the Latin grammar. Frequently he kept a fellow apprentice awake to hear him recite. He usually had to work until ten or eleven o'clock in the winter evenings, and after going to bed he would study an hour or two. In this way he acquired much of his education.

"Being a good penman, he was frequently employed to copy records and other instruments; in this way he obtained, from time to time, a little money, which he would lay out in books. He set a high standard for himself; how far he attained it his life shows.

"Perhaps you may say I have given a partial view of his character, that there might have been traits not so lovely. I was most intimately acquainted with him, both in the family and the shop; and during our acquaintance, I never heard him slander any one, or use a profane word, or tell an untruth."

I have received another communication from a cousin of the Rockwoods, who remembers distinctly his life at that time.

"I recollect," she says, "on visiting the family in August, I was asked to go out and see Thomas's garden. He had selected a position the best adapted for the purpose, and had worked extra hours upon it. His vegetables were abundant, and of the best quality. He sold nothing, and all he raised he gave away.

"The District school was taught by the Rev. Mr. Farnsworth, who told me that Sherwin was marked out for a scholar. When he was visiting in the family, allusion was made to Mr. Cummings, who went from the Clothiers Mill to College.* Thomas was much excited, and asked all manner of questions relating to Cummings and his course. Mr. Farnsworth said, 'Tom Sherwin, will go there too!'"

These statements plainly show his characteristics at that time; industry, love of knowledge, and

---

* Mr. Cummings was a graduate from Cambridge in 1801, and afterwards became an extensive publisher, of the well-known firm of Messrs. Cummings & Hilliard.

reverence for truth. In spite of every obstacle, he was always pre-eminent, often putting questions which the teachers could not answer, and puzzling his way in advance of their knowledge.

It required no superhuman power to predict that such a mind would triumph over every impediment.

Aspirations for a collegiate education grew more and more strong, until his determination became an absorbing motive. He had commenced his apprenticeship at Groton, in 1813. He continued at his employment six years, when, in his twentieth year, another person took his place in the mill; from which period he devoted his whole time to study. "My father," he says, " proposed to assist me according to his means; but as he had a sufficiently hard task to support his daughters, I chose to work through my apprenticeship, and rely upon my own efforts for an education. This resolution I have never regretted."

During the winter of 1819, he taught a district school in Harvard; in April 1820, he entered the academy at Groton. "The following March" (he says, in a manuscript from which I quote), "I went to New Ipswich academy, where I continued until I entered college, in 1821. I thus had fifteen or sixteen months for preparatory study. Within that time, I lost six or eight weeks by a fever, and taught the Central School in

Groton for three months. It is needless to say," he modestly adds, "that my qualifications for college were quite meagre, especially as my teachers were unable to render any efficient aid in case of difficulty." In 1821, he passed honorably his examination, and became a member of Harvard University. While an undergraduate, to defray his expenses, he taught school one winter in Groton, one in Leominster, and in 1825 he took charge of the academy in Lexington. Thus was he unconsciously preparing himself, in the best possible manner, for the work in which, through after life, he was to become distinguished. The same characteristics which were perceptible afterwards were noticeable here; fertile in expedients, in one instance, wishing to teach astronomy, he constructed with his own hands a globe. During this time, as subsequently, he drew the young about him with affection, and was remembered by them ever after with lasting gratitude.

I have a letter from Mr. A. F. Lawrence, of Groton, who knew him at the mill and in college. I will extract but one paragraph. He says: " Our acquaintance ripened into lasting friendship. While at the academy, he and I constituted a class (if two may be called a class) in natural philosophy, geometry, trigonometry, surveying, and astronomy. We were much together in the social circle and elsewhere. His tastes, habits, and principles, in boyhood and early manhood, were the prototype of his future life and character."

At college, in a class which included men of marked ability, among whom were Rev. Francis Cunningham, the Hon. Charles Francis Adams, Admiral Davis, Rev. Dr. Hedge, Rev. Dr. Lothrop, Dr. Augustus A. Gould, Allen Putnam, C. K. Dilloway, and Judge Ames, it was something that he could sustain himself, with the credit which he did, and that he actually graduated among the ten best scholars of his class. Mr. Sherwin was a room-mate with Augustus A. Gould, afterwards so widely known both as a Physician and Naturalist, and their friendship continued through life. They both came from New Ipswich, country boys, simple and unsophisticated, with a determination to acquire the knowledge for which they came. Sherwin, to help himself in his way through college, held the position of what was then known as "Regent's Freshman." Among the services required of him was ringing the college bell for morning and evening prayers, with other duties of a similar character.

During his college course he had a severe illness, from which his classmates never expected him to recover. His friend, Allen Putnam, watched by his bedside day and night, leaving nothing undone in his ministrations of love; and perhaps we all owe to that tender care the years of usefulness which have followed. Mr. Sherwin never ceased to remember with gratitude that watchfulness, and their continued friendship was one of the treasured facts of his life. On the most critical night, when the disease was at its height, Putnam was watching by his side, with eyes fixed upon his friend. "Why do you look so earnestly at *me*," said Sherwin; "do you fear that I shall not recover? Perhaps I shall not; but, either way" (he continued, with perfect tranquillity), "it will be all right."

I have received a communication from his classmate, C. K. Dilloway, from which I gladly extract the following: —

"Sherwin entered college older than the rest of us, and had all the characteristics of mature life. He went there to gain an education by hard study, and nobly did he do it. As a mathematical scholar, he had no superior in the class. In the classics, though laboring under the disadvantage of a brief and imperfect preparation for college, he managed to keep himself among the foremost scholars; and this in a class somewhat distinguished for mathematical and classical proficiency. His social qualities were such as would naturally make him popular and respected. He was independent in the expression of his opinions, and firm in his opposition to anything like a violation of college discipline. Our class had its full share of young men of mischievous tendency, whose influence, even over well-disposed members, was great. Sherwin turned from these, and cautioned us against them. His prudent counsels saved us from many a foolish enterprise and its consequent penalties. He was one of the most industrious men in the class, and had as little unemployed time as any man I ever knew. He worked, on an average, sixteen hours out of the twenty-four. Sherwin was then, as he was always after, a progressive man, — each year of his life seeming better than its predecessor."

This testimony of his college-days is in harmony with all I have been able to gather from his various classmates now living, and all who knew him. We see the same solid sense and sterling integrity. He was, throughout, methodical and persevering, possessing a character of such lucid purity that in him there was actually nothing one would wish to forget. It is stated by those who knew him during his college studies, as well as in his earlier days and through after years, that they never heard him use an epithet or repeat a story which could suggest an unworthy thought.

He graduated with honor in 1825. The college government, in 1827, gave proof of the high estimation in which he was held by appointing him tutor of mathematics. This office he filled acceptably for one year; when, though urged to retain it, he relinquished it for other pursuits.

A quarter of a century after, each member of the class to which he belonged gave an account in writing of what he had been doing in that time. These papers were read at the class-meeting, July, 1850.

The manuscript, written by Mr. Sherwin, is before me, and I quote his own words: "The year subsequent to leaving college, I taught the academy at Lexington, and the next year officiated as tutor in mathematics at our Alma Mater. My design at that time was to become a lawyer, and for that end I read Blackstone and part of Coke, with Elias Phinney, of Charlestown; but the prospect appearing rather barren for me, I then chose engineering, which I commenced, in 1827, with Col. Loammi Baldwin, under whom I was employed on the dry-dock and other works, at Charlestown and at Portsmouth. In September, 1827, I commenced a survey with Mr. James Hayward, for the Boston and Providence railroad; but having advanced as far as Sharon, I was attacked by a fever, which left me with pulmonary affections, and obliged me to relinquish the business. In December, 1828, I opened a private school for boys, in Boston, which, with tolerable success, I continued for one year; at the expiration of which I was elected sub-master of the English High School."

Thus, at the age of twenty-eight, we find him still contending with, and overcoming difficulties. Suddenly, the acute attack of fever threatened to bring his career to a speedy termination. But, as we have seen, he was not a person to be easily discouraged. And now that we can look back upon the space of forty years, crowded with usefulness, do we not see the hand of Providence directing him into the path he was to follow?

It is worthy of observation how much he accomplished by reasonable out-of-door exercise, and a thoughtful adaptation to physical laws. The confinement of a school-room, with its multifarious obligations, combined with the sedentary tendencies of a student's life, would not seem conducive to continued robust health to one with decided pulmonary symptoms; yet, by his wise course of life, he gained the advantages of a vigorous constitution, enjoying, in full measure, almost uninterrupted health through nearly half a century.

When Mr. Sherwin, in 1828, was elected sub-master of the High School, that institution was under the charge of S. P. Miles. He, who taught the country-boy at the parsonage, who had been his mathematical teacher while in College, was still to be his friend and associate. Through nine years there was between these two an unbroken friendship.

They were men of a kindred spirit, cheerful and conscientious; thorough scholars, and wise disciplinarians. The High School has been greatly favored in having been under the guidance of two such men. Indeed, the three head masters of the English High School — George B. Emerson, Solomon P. Miles and Thomas Sherwin—were all teachers of the highest order. They were all brought up in the country, where they were familiar with farming and rural pursuits. They were alike teachers of district schools and academies before and after their college course. They each officiated, for a time, as tutors of mathematics and natural philosophy in the University, while Mr. Sherwin had the additional advantage of learning a trade before he entered College, and, at least for a brief season, of acting as a civil and naval engineer afterwards. Multitudes of graduates throughout the country recall with joy and gratitude the influence received from these three admirable men.

Mr. Miles resigned his office as principal in 1837, when Mr. Sherwin was unanimously elected to fill the place.

Mr. Sherwin was married, June 10th, 1836, to Mary King Gibbons, daughter of Daniel L. and Mary Gibbons, of Boston, and it was the general remark that a more beautiful couple were not to be seen in the whole Commonwealth. Certain it is that a truer devotion on the part of both to the best interest and highest happiness of each could not be found. Gentle, considerate, and thoughtful, his excellences in her were more mildly reflected; while, with this, there was united all of his truthfulness, aspiration, and goodness. Happy in themselves, they helped to make all around them happy, and their home became the centre of Christian charities, as it was truly the abode of every Christian grace.

For some thirty years his residence was in the country, where his pleasant home, surrounded by an acre or two of ground, cultivated by his own hand, gave him refreshment and vigor before and after the duties connected with his school. Working in the field and garden was always a delight to him.

5

With his love of Nature, doubly endeared by early associations, the country was an unfailing resource. There he found a healing quiet which existed nowhere else. Never were his duties in the city neglected or abridged to the slightest degree, rather were they pursued with more hearty alacrity.

As proof of his resolute determination, and the fact that living in the country could not keep him from his duty, I will mention the circumstance that on a winter's morning, after one of those old-fashioned snow storms which thoroughly block up every avenue, railroads were useless, and no vehicle, of any description, could be obtained to bring him to the city. He was ten miles distant, but, unintimidated, he started on foot, beating his way through almost impassable snow-drifts, walking at times upon the top of stone walls, till at length he conquered every difficulty, and was welcomed with enthusiasm in the midst of his boys.

The ability which distinguished Mr. Sherwin as a teacher from the beginning, and which suggested his appointment to this eminent position, was manifested by that increasing success which more than justified the most sanguine expectation of his friends. It was the estimate of Mr. Tillinghast, Principal of the Normal School, at Bridgewater, that, next to the thoroughness of West Point, the Boston High School, beyond question, ranked first in the country. This commendation was corroborated by the impartial testimony of Mr. Fraser, who was appointed in England to visit the schools of this country and report to the British Parliament. In his official statement, he says: "Taking it for all in all, and as accomplishing the end at which it professes to aim, the English High School struck me as the model school of the United States. I wish," he emphatically adds, " we had a hundred such in England."

These expressions are in conformity with the public verdict.

But Mr. Sherwin's influence was never limited to the school-room. There was a breadth of purpose, as well as of view, which always characterized him. His interest in and influence over other teachers was remarkable. Desiring, in every possible way, to promote their welfare, he was prompt to engage in any duty which would diffuse light. Thus was he constantly rendering valuable service to the cause of education. He was one of the originators, in 1830, of the American Institute of Instruction. In 1853–4 he was its President. At various times he delivered able addresses, and presented important papers, while for thirty years he was one of its most efficient working officers. So also in the organization of the Massachusetts State Teachers' Association, he was one of the leading minds and most active workers; being its earliest Vice-President, and its third President. He read, on successive years, instructive lectures, and was always ready to perform needed service.

In 1847, he helped to establish " the Massachusetts Teacher," as an educational journal for the advancement of sound learning and the extension of the best methods of promoting the cause of education. He was an active member of the publishing committee, was one of the original editors, and for a long time had charge of its mathematical department.

For the benefit of teachers, there was no labor he was not willing to perform. " The legitimate object of a teacher's exertions," he would say, " is to make mankind wiser, purer, truer, holier. To feel that we have rescued one individual from a life of ignorance and vice, is more true and lasting glory than to have worn a crown."

This was to him no mere sound of words. It was the faith which bound him to his profession, and which powerfully attracted him to the whole company of teachers who were engaged in the same calling. " There exists between us," he would say, " a bond of sympathy stronger than friendship; we are engaged in a common cause; a cause second to none in importance, inferior to none in its bearing ,upon the destinies of the world."

"No one who is not willing," he said to a company of instructors, "no one who is not willing to labor perseveringly, and with his whole might, should ever desecrate the business of teaching. The great work of education is a stern reality. It admits of no compromise with evil, and no sacrifice of duty. It is sublime and boundless as human capabilities. It is well, therefore, that we strive to improve ourselves in all that embellishes and strengthens, in all that purifies and extends, the sway we may exert."

Few could know better than he did, how arduous and wearing are the duties of a faithful teacher; the unremitting exertion, the frequent perplexity, and the exhausting care to which he must be subjected; but he knew, also, that the desired result is worth it all; that there can be no field of duty bearing more directly in its consequences upon the public welfare, and that with proper methods and a right spirit, the burdens of the teacher's toil will be lightened, and his mind cheered, while he will have the unspeakable satisfaction of feeling that he is fulfilling the will of God, and becoming, in the truest sense, a benefactor of mankind.

In the language of Mr. Sherwin, "It is a great mistake to suppose, because we know more than time, opportunity, and the capacity of our scholars will enable us to impart, that therefore our usefulness is not augmented by increasing our attainments. Every accession of knowledge will give the teacher increased skill and facility in imparting information."

His acquired resources, "he must remould to his own mind, adapting them to his special wants and opportunities; endeavoring to make them productive of the greatest good in his particular sphere of usefulness."

Deeply interested in children, and truly loving his work, "he should take pleasure in earnest endeavors to do good, although the immediate fruit may not fully answer his expectations. He should be delighted by the new acquisitions which his pupils make, rather than become disheartened by their comparative ignorance; he must rejoice at the development of the true and the good in their characters, rather than be discouraged by manifestations of evil; and at the close of each day's labor, he should be able to console himself for having accomplished so little, by the consciousness that he has endeavored to do his best; feeling confident that the minutest seed which he has caused to germinate may yet grow up into a noble tree."

"The teacher," he says, " without losing a consciousness of his own superiority, should aim to throw himself as much as possible into the mind of the child, to
sympathize with him in his emotions and his difficulties." He calls upon the teacher "to gather fresh im-
pulses to duty, new vigor and alacrity; to gain added
materials for illustration, and stronger motives for
exertion. He who goes abroad with his powers of
observation awake and active, will derive much from
what he sees and hears that will be of advantage in
the instruction of others." All this, he maintains,
"will impart to the teacher new happiness, and especially enlarge his power of usefulness."

To enforce the importance of a continued youthful
vivacity on the part of an instructor, he says that " a
peach-tree at Montreuil, in France, was in full bearing at the age of fifty years, and capable of produ-
cing annually ten or twelve bushels of fruit. This
great degree of vigor and longevity was effected,
he adds, by pruning away the barren and cumbrous
parts, and growing, in their stead, new and fertile
shoots; in fact, the whole secret consisted in keeping
the tree constantly young. May not a teacher, he
asks, do something analogous; keeping himself constantly young, and in a fruit-bearing condition?" To
this inquiry, Mr. Sherwin's own life is at once the
most convincing answer and happy illustration.

"The influence we may and must exert," he writes,
"either for good or evil, is such as to demand all
possible exertion to qualify ourselves for the faithful
and successful performance of our duties. The ripple
marks of the antediluvian waves, the impress of rain-
drops which fell prior to the existence of man, even
the foot-prints of the wind, that swept over the face
of the uninhabited waste, remain stamped in the ada-
mantine rock, and present a meteorological journal
almost as accurate as that traced by the pen of the
philosopher within the current year. So the impress
of our exertions, what we teach, whether by precept
or example, our successes and our failures, will be
transmitted to generations, thousands of years hence,
and remain indelibly inscribed upon the various strata
of human life."

Such were his views of the teacher's work. A calling which, as he contemplated it, was full of grandeur.
No minister of the Gospel was more absolutely an
ambassador of heaven, and the stateliest cathedral in
Europe was not more truly a temple of God, than the
school-room in which he taught. His work to him
was a sacred ministry. He commenced his labors each
morning in the school-room with extemporaneous
prayer, and entered upon all his labors as one bap-
tized in the pure fountain of eternal love.

"Seneca, Socrates, Plato," he said, "were teachers; yes, and our Lord and Saviour was the Great Teacher."

As an expression of some of his general views, I quote from a letter I received from him, dated April, 1865:

"We spend too much time on *vehicles* of knowledge, to have sufficient time for knowledge itself. This is the great defect in the education of England. The same evil has been fostered among us. The opposite error is to make Education wholly subservient to what is called business,—as if it were more important to insure success in the affairs of life, than to make true men and women. Language, the artificial and somewhat arbitrary contrivance of man, should, by no means, be neglected. But who can, with truth, say that the great book of nature, bearing the impress of infinite power, wisdom, and goodness is of secondary importance? A teacher should know every thing and be everything that is good. But as these are rather high qualifications, we must be content with only moderate approximations. Deficiency in the knowledge of natural science is too common among teachers. I trust we are taking the initial steps to remedy

6

this deficiency. I have often thought that a good knowledge of chemistry, geology, zoölogy, and botany is a better qualification for a teacher in the school under my charge, than perfect familiarity with all the Latin and Greek that was ever written. '*In modo* is much, but *in re* is vastly more.'"

His love for nature and the natural sciences gained strength through advancing years. "Education must be changed," he would say, "to correspond with the progress of society."

"The great book of nature, glowing all over with characters of living light, affords arguments inexhaustible, and illustrations without number. No one who has made the natural sciences a study, can fail to perceive the moral and religious instruction they afford. The question is whether we should not take more pains to show the young what God has done for them, in this beautiful world of ours."

In a letter I received from Mr. Sherwin's son, he says: —

"Every insect, leaf, and flower was to him an illustration of the omnipotence and wisdom of the Almighty. There was no creature so small, or so despised, that he was not ready to find a claim for its existence. Had leisure been granted, from the earnest work in which his life was spent, he would have been an ardent naturalist. He was a religious man, not only from faith, but through processes of intellectual thought. If he had been debarred from every study but his favorite one of mathematics, the pursuit of that alone, and the great and, to him, divine laws which govern the exact sciences, would have led him to a belief in God. In the acquisition of knowledge, he sought to apply the principles already mastered to the great problems of nature, science, and philosophy, to which all study leads, as the movements of a single planet are but in obedience to, and part of, the great plan of the universe; so he regarded every branch of study as part of that grand inquiry for truth which ends only with the Infinite."

In 1854, at the opening of the American Institute of Instruction, of which Mr. Sherwin was president, he said: "The lapse of twenty-five years, since we commenced, has blanched the locks of many among us, but we trust it has not deadened our zeal, nor abated our interest in the holy cause of education."

We may be sure that time had produced no such influence upon him; his character during a quarter of a century had but grown more mellow, and his zeal more strong.

In May, 1836, he was elected a member of the American Academy of Arts and Sciences; in which Society, for more than thirty years, he continued an active interest. In February, 1868, he was chosen a member of the New England Historic Genealogical Society. And from the first organization of the Institute of Technology, he was a director; for the past ten years, attending its evening meetings, and faithfully laboring for its advancement.

In addition to communications and lectures, read and printed through successive years, he published two works on Algebra which are the best text-books upon this subject used in our schools. For clearness of thought and conciseness of expression, for judicious selection and wise adaptation to the mind of the learner, they are not surpassed by any school-books ever written.

Horace Mann, when Secretary of the Board of Education, stated that attention was given to Algebra in less than one hundred towns of the State; in not one half of the seventy-eight incorporated academies was Algebra studied, and in those instances only by a few scholars. When we consider that this study has now become nearly universal, and that Mr. Sherwin's book has been adopted, almost without exception, as the standard authority, we have reason to infer that the author has greatly helped to extend an important branch of education; and that, by what he has thus done, he has rendered a public service.

In addition to his partiality for the natural sciences and for mathematics, Mr. Sherwin had a decided fondness for languages. He spoke and read French fluently, and was well versed in French literature. He understood and could teach Spanish. He had knowledge of German, and read Latin with ease. Livy and Cicero were favorite authors, while Horace often gained a share of his more leisure hours.

Mr. G. H. Lodge, for many years his intimate friend, writes as follows: "Mr. Sherwin was an industrious student, an honest thinker, a calm reasoner, mild and tolerant. Through a series of years, we met on successive weeks at each other's rooms. We studied German, French, and Spanish together. We played duets on the flute. We discussed questions on the arts, grammar, etc. Our intercourse was very happy, and I think the better of myself for having been the friend of Thomas Sherwin."

Mr. Sherwin's reading took a wide range. He was familiar with all the standard histories and most of the English classics. He had read the older

French authors and dramatists, as well as all the works upon mathematics which could be obtained, — many of the latter so abstruse and difficult that few men in the country would think of taking them up, yet he read them for amusement and relaxation. He was a great admirer of Shakspeare and Milton. The works of Prescott, Macaulay, and Motley he knew intimately, and fully kept up to the times on all topics of thought and inquiry. He read with interest the writings of Sir Walter Scott and Charles Dickens, though he felt a little annoyed that in delineating the character of the Teacher, they had both done something to bring the profession he himself so honored into ridicule and disrepute. The leading periodicals, — American, English and French, — which he thought well-informed men should be acquainted with, he read quite extensively.

Such were his scholarly tastes and habits.

There were but few objects upon which he did not make himself intelligently conversant. He was acquainted with practical Farming, knew the characteristics and capabilities of different soils, the proper succession of crops, the chemical properties of the atmosphere and the earth. He had read the best works on agriculture, and had gained much information on the same subject, both from personal experience and intercourse with others. In Architecture he felt keenly sensitive to any defects, and an appreciative admiration for all that was good. His mathematical knowledge ministered to his artistic tastes. Upon the subject of Music he professed much information; without pretending to profound scientific knowledge, he had a correct ear and cultivated taste, while compositions of the highest order he could both analyze and enjoy.*

Indeed, his ever-active mind lost no reasonable opportunity of gaining knowledge, while all that he acquired was made subservient to the interests of education. He would often say, " I can make this of service to my boys."

Thus was there a constant self-culture and growth. His pupils often felt, as many others did also, that he was an encyclopædia of information. No opportunity with him, either of gaining or imparting, was neglected. When the drawing master came to teach

---

* As an indication of the versatility of his gifts, and that he had in his nature the poetic element combined with a fine sense of wit and humor, it may be mentioned that about two years since he prepared for a meeting of his college classmates a poem of nearly one hundred and fifty lines, into which he most ingeniously introduced the name of every member of the class, with graphic descriptions and amusing characteristics, " which kept," to use the language of one present, " the whole company in a roar of laughter."

the classes, he would take a seat with the boys, and draw by their side. When Professor Munroe went through the vocal exercises, and gymnastic drill, he would gladly participate. He never became too old to learn, or lost his enthusiasm for improvement. So affairs went on prosperously in the history of the school. The path of duty quietly pursued, and always with continued progress.

But at length a great change came over the whole country. An ominous cloud spread its tempestuous shadow! Many were appalled by dark forebodings. Treacherous and malignant hands threatened the very life of the nation. The slave oligarchy, filled with insane ambition, laid its plans deeply, and with a crafty cunning. Thoroughly loyal himself, what he saw filled him with indignation and grief. Every act of perfidy and treason roused him the more. The outbreak of hostilities, the cruelty to our men, — all stirred his heart. What would he not do for his country? He attended public meetings, encouraged effort, and liberally contributed money, to the full extent of his means. He rejoiced as he heard of past graduates of the school, springing, on every side, to the aid of the national government. By word, look, and deed, he helped the good cause. With him there was no lukewarmness. The cause of our armies was the cause of humanity and of God.

He was deeply interested in the formation of the first colored regiment (the 54th Massachusetts), and raised a large sum for its equipment.

But more than this. Providence had blessed him with three sons, — all the children he had, and these three manly young men, — which of them could he give to this great cause? He gave them all. Yes, from that pleasant, peaceful home, three courageous, patriotic men went forth, ready, if need be, to die. Two entered the navy, and did their work there, fearlessly and well. And one joined the volunteers of the United States Army, going out as an officer in the 22d Massachusetts. For three years, serving in the army of the Potomac, he was in more than twenty battles, and, after being wounded in the service, he again returned to his regiment. He rose to be Lieutenant-Colonel, and was afterwards brevetted Brigadier General.

Among the honored men who did service to the country through that trying period, and whose courage and fidelity helped to crown our cause with success, should ever be remembered with gratitude, General Thomas Sherwin.

7

When at length, through the devoted heroism of our soldiery, the skill of our commanders, and the wisdom of the executive, victory, by a kind Providence, with succeeding peace and prosperity, were granted to the nation, Mr. Sherwin found himself, thank Heaven, reunited to his three sons. While thousands had fallen, they had been preserved. Now the country was safe. The integrity of the national government had been vindicated. A colossal evil, the root of all our woe, existed no longer; and a glorious future was opening before us. Mr. Sherwin felt the weight of anxiety lifted from his mind. His natural cheerfulness returned to him, and he seemed, as he indeed was, one of the happiest of men.

In the midst of all this tranquillity, with joy and peace around him, a cherished dream of his life seemed about to be realized. The thought of a visit to Europe had naturally floated before him. The scenes associated so intimately with his reading and study; interwoven with history, science and art ; the monuments of past ages, the footprints of civilization, — even a hasty glance at these would not only be a great personal gratification, but would aid him in the education of others.

What fresh illustrations it would furnish! What added power it might impart! Thirty years of incessant labor was beginning to wear upon him; a few months' absence might invigorate both body and mind. The committee granted leave of absence, and everything seemed auspicious.

As an indication of his feelings, I read the following words, which I received in a note written by him at that time : —

"The English High School," he says, "is, after my own family, my great, almost my only object of interest in this life. I shall leave it, even for a short time, with feelings of reluctance. I hope and trust, however, that it will not suffer by my absence, and that on my return, it may be benefitted by the knowledge obtained from a wider observation of the world than I have hitherto enjoyed."

Such were his views and feelings. Arrangements were nearly completed; he was to accompany his friend and relative, the Hon. Marshall P. Wilder. The passage was engaged; when, a few days before the steamer was to leave, a sudden impediment presented itself. A newly appointed teacher had found difficulty in the management of his charge. The boys refused to be controlled. The teacher had lost confidence, and was overpowered. Mr. Sherwin called

at my house. I said, "I am rejoiced to see you."
He replied, "You will not be, when you know why
I am here." "What, then," I said, "is the occasion?" He replied, "Trouble." He stated the par-
ticulars, adding, "What am I to do? My plans
are laid, my passage taken, but I cannot go. It will
not answer. Am I right?"

There he stood, true to his duty, true to himself.
The thought of Europe, with all its attractions, just
within his reach, the cherished dream of his life
about to be realized. Could he leave his school, even
if one department was in a state of insubordination?
Not for a moment could he hesitate. His duty was
here. Every plan was instantly changed; and
from that hour he continued at his post.

This was a simple, natural, truthful illustration of
the man. It was in harmony with his course through
forty years. His whole soul was in his work; and in
this instance, great as the disappointment was, he
would hardly allow himself to call it disappointment
while duty demanded him here.

He thought then it was possible he might go
abroad at some future time; but that time never came.
Cheerfully he gave himself to his accustomed labors.
Harmony was at once restored, and the whole school
displayed a proficiency and progress which had not
been surpassed.

The English High School, whose origin had formed an era in the educational history of the city, was intended to afford the very best practical education which could possibly be obtained. Mr. Sherwin's strenuous purpose, from the beginning, was to make this school, in every particular, all that it professed to be; and not only so, but to carry it forward to yet higher attainments, embracing whatever was most valuable in the advancing tendencies of the times.

For three grand results this school, under the guidance of Mr. Sherwin, became justly distinguished.

First. For *thoroughness.* Whatever was acquired, was understood. Every principle involved was rendered so clear that it could not but be comprehended. Nothing essential was slighted; nothing superficial was tolerated. A tutor in Harvard University informed me that he could readily designate the graduates of this school, from any other students in the college, by the accuracy of their acquirements, and by their complete mastery of whatever studies they had pursued.

Second. The *development of mental power.* Mr. Sherwin taught his pupils to think for themselves. Not contented with imparting information, he quickened and unfolded the faculties, arousing the whole intellect into healthy and vigorous activity. Teaching every capacity not only to work, but how to work to the best possible advantage.

Third. *Manliness of character.* Integrity of thought; self-reliance, and self-respect; the best type of a noble Manhood. Principle, not blind impulse or a temporizing policy, but a deep-rooted love for the right, the true, and the good. No amount of knowledge, without these, could satisfy Mr. Sherwin; they were to him the consummation to which all education should tend.

It was the power which Mr. Sherwin possessed to inspire this spirit and secure these results, which led so many of the young men to become heartily attached to him while under his care, and to pursue, through after years, a career of undeviating usefulness. In professional life, in mercantile business, and amid the wearing pursuits of daily toil, they proved themselves, in the best sense, honorable citizens, and in many instances became widely recognized as benefactors of society.

Teachers and graduates, shall we step, for an instant, into the school-room, and glance at the method of teaching which left such results?

How striking is that presence! The calm and intellectual expression; those finely chiselled features; the firm decision of the mouth; the quiet yet commanding deportment; unaffected dignity, blended with manly grace.

It is the hour of recitation. We hear not the formal interchange of questions and answers, mechanically repeated from a text-book, — far different; how natural the unfolding of the subject, how animated the thought, with illustrations from nature and from life, awakening in each mind the interest of personal discovery!

When the teacher speaks, how marked is his brevity! Every expression exactly to the point, with never a syllable too little or too much. Good Saxon words, and of those the shortest and simplest. Like Porson, he condescends to call a spade a spade, and not a horticultural implement. How often, with one sentence, he sends a blaze of light over the whole subject, making its meaning clear as day. Old Chaucer described him, five centuries ago, when, in his Canterbury Pilgrim, he says: —

> " Not a word spake he, more than was need;
> And that was said in form and reverence,
> And short and quick, and full of high sentence:
> Sounding in moral virtue was his speech,
> And gladly would he learn, and gladly teach."

In mathematics, navigation, astronomy, mechanics, the black-board is constantly in requisition. Each proposition is demonstrated in every part, and this not by four or five of the brightest boys, but by every boy in the class. Nothing is taken for granted, and nothing is left unillustrated or unexplained.

Beyond the regular instruction, observe from time to time, and always at the right instant, what wise counsel and pithy advice, — not prosaic moralizing, but a concise and happy statement, graphic as Franklin's, full of that shrewdness and sound sense which gains for it a cordial welcome, and causes it to bear fruit through after years.

Numerous instances might be mentioned of the felicitous manner in which items of practical advice were given, to be of service in the future experience of actual life. Our friend and associate, Mr. Charles F. Wyman, recalls the manner in which he urged the habit of keeping a strict account of personal expenses. "Some of you," said Mr. Sherwin, "may have little, if any, spending-money; others may be more favored; but be the amount less or more, you will do well to keep an account-book. Not that I would have you become mean or selfish by such a course; but you will probably thus secure to yourselves habits of order and proper economy. But I recommend this plan especially because most of you will be engaged in mercantile pursuits, and if you learn to take care of your own money, you will thus save yourselves much labor and temptation in the care you have over the property of your employers." There were young men in that class who cordially received that wise suggestion, and have faithfully acted upon it from that day, and who have found its value increase with every year. It was probably not so much what was said, as the manner in which it was said, which gave to this simple and timely advice such an enduring influence.

So also Mr. Simpson recalls the fact that one morning during the war, the pupils and teacher were much excited over the news of battles just fought, in which near relatives of those present were doubtless engaged, when suddenly Mr. Sherwin exclaimed, kindly yet emphatically, " Well, boys, the army will attend to *its* duty *there, our* duty lies *here.*" That expression, so given, the pupils declare, always recurs to their minds when they are tempted at any time to neglect the duty immediately before them. Those words seem still audible: " *Our* duty lies *here.*"

Mr. Moriarty, the faithful secretary of the High

8

School Association, recalls another impressive incident. One morning, Mr. Sherwin's manner was unusually solemn. After the opening morning exercise, he addressed the class. "My young friends," he said, " you are in the morning of life, and have, before you, I trust, many years of prosperity. I am in the evening of my days, and know not how many years Providence may have in store for me. But whatever these years might be, I would gladly relinquish them all, if, by so doing, I could render service to my country. Were a gulf to open at my feet, filled with blazing fire, and I knew that by plunging into it, I could spare my country the ordeal through which she is passing, I would not hesitate to do so."

His earnest expression of countenance, the impressive tones of his voice, showed how deeply he felt all he said; and every boy there knew that he would, in very truth, have done this and more, if, by so doing, he could, in that trying hour, have benefitted his country.

With Mr. Sherwin no fraction of the day was misspent. He did not waste three-fourths of his time in striving to ascertain how he should dispose of the other fourth to advantage. No one knew better than he did how to make the utmost of each moment as it came. No slight proportion of his power came from his promptitude.

So also with regard to discipline, his thoughtful consideration prevented the necessity of severe measures. For more than twenty years, not a blow had been struck. Courtesy and kindness led to obedience and respect; and this was secured by personal dignity and weight of character. In a note I received from him upon this subject, he says: "Interest a scholar in what is useful, purifying, elevating, and you acquire almost necessarily a sufficient control over him." "If," he adds, "a scholar realizes that the teacher is deeply interested in his welfare, that good order and the scrupulous observance of rules are essential to that welfare, and if with this knowledge, the pupil is kept fully employed, he will rarely prove troublesome." He endeavored to place a boy where his antagonistic feelings would not become excited; to work with his nature rather than against it. Sir Walter Scott once said that if he knew a man had several pounds of gunpowder in his pocket, he did not precisely understand why he need insist upon that man's taking his seat next to the fire. When Mr. Sherwin knew that a lad was composed of combustible material, he placed him where the least harm might be anticipated. He knew how to

avoid evil, by putting out of the way the causes
which lead to it; and he knew how to encourage
and strengthen what was good, by establishing all
those conditions which tend thither. He pre-occu-
pied the mind by what was right; and kindled within
it such true purposes, that all its interests and tendencies turned instinctively in that direction.

If any wrong disposition was discovered, he had
his own way of meeting it,— seldom administering
rebuke before others, in a manner to create bitterness
of feeling. His method, in each instance, was individual, and adapted to the particular circumstances. It
might be difficult to describe such a case, it depended
so greatly upon his own peculiar manner.

A lad was guilty of falsehood. Mr. Sherwin called
him up, but instead of punishment, or even direct re-
proof, he broke forth into an enthusiastic exposition
of truth,— the value of truth, the beauty of truth, the
majesty of truth. His mind kindled with his theme,
and this boy, standing there, without one syllable of
censure, seemed as if in the midst of a consuming fire.
Remorse seized upon him, and he burst into a flood
of tears. His companions declare that from that hour
they never knew him to be guilty of an untruth.

Mr. Sherwin was quick to discern and appreciate
every honest effort; and such was his evident sympa-

thy with his pupils, that he readily commanded their confidence. They did not need to be told that he cared for them, every look and word proved it. He never despaired of a boy, or gave one up as hopeless. "Can we not do something with him?" was the question he asked; and when some latent faculty was discovered, or some motive of action to which an effective appeal could be made, with what sincere gratification would he lead the boy on from one field of inquiry and another, feeling amply rewarded for every effort if he could thus secure all the improvement which the nature of the case rendered possible.

Boys who become disheartened and discouraged under the charge of other teachers, by such judicious treatment went through an intellectual regeneration. Many a pupil, by his care, has experienced the most wonderful transformation, and acknowledged in after years, with tears of gratitude, the deep indebtedness due to him.

There was an entire absence of partiality. Favoritism in his presence was a thing unthought of; — absolute justice was extended to all. The truest welfare of every one, they knew, he had at heart. A lad who was a cripple, exclaimed : "He is the best man I ever knew." A colored young man, who received a medal for excellency in declamation, and a diploma for honorable proficiency in his studies, said to me : "He treats us all with equal kindness, and a generous care which knows no bounds."

In order to adapt himself the better to the wants of each individual, he took pains to acquaint himself with the antecedents of all, — their history, home, and social surroundings. If they were ill, he would visit them. If they were destitute, in the most delicate way he would minister to their necessities.

When they were about to leave his more immediate care, he would endeavor to gain for them desirable places. Hundreds through him have secured advantageous positions; and even after this he kept himself acquainted with their plans and prospects. Such was the confidence in his judgment, that business houses would consult him, making application for young men. And those who had been under his care, after they had entered into business relations, would still come to him for advice and to express their gratitude.

Well did President Wayland affirm that the work of education " presents subjects vast enough, and interests grave enough, to task the highest efforts of the most gifted intellect, in the full vigor of its powers." Such were Mr. Sherwin's views of education. In this spirit he entered upon his duties, and with the same spirit he continued to the end.

The Rev. Dr. Lothrop, Mr. Sherwin's college classmate and friend, — the efficient chairman of the committee on the English High School, and whose important services in behalf of education are well known, — writes to me as follows: "For the last twenty years, my personal and official relations with Mr. Sherwin have been most intimate, and always the great feature I have noticed was growth. Every year he was a better, broader, more tolerant and scholarly man. There was a reality about him, a freedom from arrogance and pretence, show and routine, rarely found in a man who has devoted forty years to the profession of teaching. He taught in a variety of departments, yet in every one he was in advance of the text-books, and no new discovery in science or inventive art, was made, but he got hold of it, knew all about it, and communicated the facts orally to his pupils, long before it could otherwise come to them. This gave a freshness and reality to his teaching alike interesting and useful to his pupils. He never did a nobler or grander work than during his last year."

Mr. Sherwin was connected with the English High School from 1828 to 1869, a period of forty-one years, during thirty of which he had the supreme charge.

Within this time, three thousand nine hundred and thirty-seven boys were enrolled as pupils of the school. Nearly four thousand young men thus came under his directing and moulding power. Who can describe the effect of such instruction and discipline upon so many destined to take active part in the practical labors and duties of life ?

The last graduating class which had the privilege of Mr. Sherwin's care, numbered forty-four. The closing exhibition took place, Saturday, July 17. Mr. Sherwin conducted the exercises. Nine pupils received Franklin medals. It was the declaration of Mr. Philbrick, that "this year of school-service was the most completely successful of any of the forty years of his connection with the school; which, he adds, "is the highest eulogy that can be pronounced upon any teacher."

The School Festival took place at the Music Hall, July 20th, at which Mr. Sherwin was present, in excellent spirits. I had, on that day, a most pleasant conversation with him, which will ever remain as a sacred remembrance.

On July 21 and 22, the examination of candidates for admission to the High School took place. There were two hundred and twenty-seven applicants examined, of whom one hundred and sixty-two were admitted. Mr. Sherwin conducted the examinations on both days, in apparently perfect health.

On the day following, being at his house in the country, he accompanied his son to the railroad station, stating, as they parted, "I shall call to consult with the physician, as I do not feel exactly right."

This was the first intimation given to any one respecting indisposition. During the consultation, he spoke of an intermittent motion of the pulse. "You have observed *that?*" said the physician. He replied, "I have."

He saw that the trouble was serious. The signal for departure had sounded, and he might be called at any moment. He continued calm and undisturbed; so much so that, shortly after, the physician happening to overtake him on his way towards home, overheard him singing to himself a pleasant tune. Thus Bunyan's Pilgrim, at the window which opened towards the rising sun, when he thought of the Celestial City and the shining ones, awoke and sang! — so little did apprehension cast its shadow over the natural serenity of his mind. After this, he united in pleasant conversation with his family, walked in the garden, went to his room, took a book, and in a moment, without a sign or struggle, passed from this life to another.

In conversation with a friend, not long before, he

had said, "When I depart, I hope it will be suddenly, like the going out of a candle." He went in accordance with his wish.

"It will make but little difference," he said to his friend, "when we go, if we are only prepared." His whole life was a preparation. He adored the wisdom and goodness of God, through his word and his works; — and glorious to him was the prospect of that immortality, in which he should behold yet more fully the ways of Jehovah.

Nay, so truly did he revere his calling, that he believed he should still be engaged much in the same way, studying truth and imparting it. "If God," he would say, "has given me such duties here, and endowed me with a capacity for them, why may there not be similar duties in a higher sphere?" Sublime and inspiring faith! True through life to the highest purpose and the divinest thought, with the same unextinguishable love of goodness and truth, his soul desired to carry even into heaven its work of usefulness!

It was in July when the last service took place. The multitude of mourners that assembled, neighbors and friends, old and young, teachers and taught, attested to the wide sense of private and public loss, and to that heartfelt reverence and love in which he was universally held.

A more faithful and useful teacher had probably not lived, from the time of Roger Ascham, to Dr. Arnold, of Rugby.

Indeed, between Mr. Sherwin and Dr. Arnold there were striking resemblances. In the character of each a strong natural capacity was united to industry, constant and unabating. Both had a sympathy for young people, with a real pleasure in the work of instruction, and an interest in that work which only increased with advancing age.

Both united firmness with tenderness, and modesty with true self-respect and personal independence.

"I hold," said Dr. Arnold, "that a man is only fit to teach so long as he is himself learning daily." No words could express more exactly the principle and practice of Mr. Sherwin.

Both were impatient of mere routine, and carried into all their labors a spirit of Life, giving freshness and flexibility to all they undertook.

They mutually discarded from the school-room, artifice and dogmatism; treating all with courtesy and kindness, and gaining in return confidence and friendship.

Both acted upon the principle that more should be done by the boys, than for them; and that the most desirable thing to teach them, was the use of their own faculties.

Both introduced into the school-room the highest principles of action, and carried the same principles fully out in their intercourse with mankind.

Neither could be narrowed down into the mere pedagogue, but stood up in the full stature of many-sided and complete manhood; fulfilling various duties for the public welfare, and striving at all times to promote the best interests of society.

They alike cultivated the habit of " doing what was right, speaking what was true, and thinking what was good."

It was not a little remarkable that while there was such a resemblance in character, there should have been so many corresponding circumstances in their external life; and that at length both should have been taken away with the same instantaneous sud-denness from the midst of active duty. Within eight or ten years, the attendance at the English High School had doubled; the number of pupils at Rugby had rapidly increased in the same manner. In each school, the term had just drawn to a close, and the graduating class had passed through their public day of valedictory exercises. The examina-tion of the new class had taken place, when both

Teachers, in the midst of apparent health, and in the full exercise of every faculty, were, by a disease of the heart, taken at once from this life into the realities of eternity.

There was throughout, an Individuality in the life we have been considering; a vital unity; an inner law of growth, which, from the beginning, developed itself, persistently to the end. Few persons ever carried out more fully that favorite sentence of Marcus Aurelius: "Let nothing be done without a purpose." To educate himself thoroughly, perfectly, in every faculty and power, might with him have been called a pervading passion; and the knowledge he craved for himself, with the truest liberality he wished all others to enjoy. With such views of life and education (on every side broad and far-reaching), his interest could never falter. The desire to teach had been the ambition of his younger days; it was the delight of his maturer life, and it continued the absorbing enjoyment of his riper age; while, through all, he became daily more learned, more wise, more capable, retaining to the last the cheerfulness, the elasticity, and the freshness of youth.

Of those teachers who were most intimately asso-

ciated with Mr. Sherwin in his direct labors, not a
few had been with him ten, fifteen, and twenty years.
Teachers of the English High School, do I not express the sentiment of your hearts when I say, that
nothing can surpass the strength of your attachment,
or the profoundness of that homage which you cherish for his memory?

With the most thoughtful kindness and true liberality, he always left you, as you will gladly testify, to
accomplish requisite results by your own methods;
encouraging you ever to cherish ideas of your own;
securing through this means the individuality of all,
while at the same time, he could hardly fail to gain
your added confidence and respect by that large and
pleasant freedom you were allowed to enjoy in the
discharge of your several duties.

His name will forever be honorably identified with
the school over which he presided so long and so well.
May his mantle, like that of the prophet Elijah, fall
upon his successors, and may the school itself not
only maintain its present high standard of excellence,
but prove, by continued progress, its capability of
meeting the enlarged demands of the coming time.

I see before me not only those who were with
him in his school, but a large representation of the

teachers of Boston, who were all bound to him by ties of personal friendship.

Teachers of Boston, natural it was that you should feel proud of such an associate. For forty years he had labored among you, with unceasing assiduity, never limiting his sympathies to his own school, but embracing in his affection the whole educational interests of the community. How could you do otherwise than honor and love him?

When I think of the five-and-thirty thousand children entrusted to your daily care; when I recall the fact that at least one hundred and twenty-five thousand pupils have received instruction in the public schools of Boston since Mr. Sherwin entered upon his duties as teacher; and that the whole of this vast number have been affected for evil or for good, by your fidelity or remissness, I am more impressed than ever by the momentous character of your work, and feel that Mr. Sherwin was right in the high estimate he put upon it.

Is there not much in the life we have been contemplating to stimulate and inspire every teacher? Mr. Philbrick, the superintendent of schools, has affirmed that "no one among us has occupied so important a position in the public service for so long a period, with such uniform and eminent success."

Many there are, I know, of rare acquirement and exalted virtue; I feel it as I look upon those who are gathered around me here. But, Teachers, where shall we look to find all the qualifications requisite for a superior teacher existing in so high a degree? Where shall we find another mind in which all the moral and intellectual qualities abound in such perfect and beautiful harmony?

May his memory throw a new sanctity over the teacher's office, and the thought of what he was, and what he did, give fresh impulse to the cause of education, both here and throughout the land.

Mr. President and officers of the High School Association, who among the four thousand scholars whose names have been enrolled as pupils of the High School since Mr. Sherwin first became connected with it, will not gladly cherish his memory? From that four thousand have gone forth men to occupy every walk of life, many of whom have risen to eminent positions in industrial pursuits, and in the public service; the city, the state, the nation, have recognized their just claims to honor. Among all those graduates there is probably not one whose heart will not throb with lasting gratitude to Mr. Sherwin; not one who will not gladly unite in the memorial which is now proposed as a fitting tribute to his memory.

We have traced Mr. Sherwin's career from his childhood to his mature age; have seen him as a lad, — at Westmoreland and at Temple, — have followed him in his apprenticeship, as he fulfilled his daily task‘ studying his book while he worked at the loom; have witnessed him, in the face of every obstacle, fitting himself for college; and, having finished his academic course with honor, we have seen him appointed tutor in the University; and afterwards, for forty years, becoming identified with all that was best in the educational interests of the city.

There might, perhaps, have been a portion of this period when his character appeared too austere; if any one ever thought so, they would have seen that character, with advancing age, rounding into beautiful harmony. As he grew older, he became younger. The cares and anxieties, which pressed upon him in his earlier days, passed away, and the more genial element shone forth with unclouded brightness.

" Be sure," said Southey, " no man was ever discontented with the world who did his duty in it." Mr. Sherwin, by his very fidelity to duty, became not only himself more cheerful, but imparted, beyond question, increased happiness to others.

10

And while zealously fulfilling his various duties, with Faith he embraced joyfully the great Future. Earth became associated with Heaven, and the light of revelation shed its beams over the whole of existence. He recognized God through all nature, and Providence through all history. These convictions were an indissoluble part of his life, — an essential essence of his being, illuminating every thought, and sending the radiance of immortal promise into boundless eternity.

Teachers of Boston, honor forever the associate who so loved the duties to which you are devoted.

Graduates of the High School, hold in grateful remembrance the teacher who so endeared himself to every generous heart.

Citizens and friends, one who stood in the foremost rank of representative men has passed away, but his influence will remain as long as his memory endures, and his memory will live while there are minds to appreciate real worth.

In the language of the ancient Scripture, " Light, and understanding, and wisdom, and knowledge, and an excellent spirit, were found in him." May the same spirit animate us all to emulate an example so noble.